THE WOMAN WHO TURNED CHILDREN INTO BIRDS

THE WOMAN WHO TURNED

DAVID ALMOND

First US edition 2022
First published by Walker Books Ltd. (UK) 2022

· · · · · · · · · · · · · · · · · · · ·

Library of Congress Catalog Card Number 2021953460
ISBN 978-1-5362-1996-8

· · · · · · · · · · · · · · · · · · · ·

APS 27 26 25 24 23 22
10 9 8 7 6 5 4 3 2 1

· · · · · · · · · · · · · · · · · · · ·

Printed in Humen, Dongguan, China

· · · · · · · · · · · · · · · · · · · ·

This book was typeset in Adobe Jenson Pro.
The illustrations were done in mixed media.

· · · · · · · · · · · · · · · · · · · ·

Candlewick Studio
an imprint of
Candlewick Press
99 Dover Street
Somerville, Massachusetts 02144

· · · · · · · · · · · · · · · · · · · ·

www.candlewickstudio.com

CHILDREN INTO BIRDS

illustrated by LAURA CARLIN

CANDLEWICK STUDIO
an imprint of Candlewick Press

A woman came to town.
Her name was Nanty Solo.
She said she could turn
children into birds.

•

"What rubbish!" said the teachers.
"There's laws against it!" said the police.
"It's just plain daft. It's total trash.
It's piffle, twaddle, balderdash."

•

"You don't want that to happen,
do you, children?
So stay away!"

But of course there was one little girl.
Her name was Dorothy Carr.
She pretended to be just wandering
and thinking of nothing at all.
Nanty Solo called to her.
"Would you like to sit with me?"
Dorothy knew that maybe she shouldn't.
But oh, she did.

Nanty made marks upon the earth.

She whispered words into Dorothy's ear.

And then she said,

"Go on. Be happy. Off you fly!"

And where there'd once been a Dorothy Carr,

there was now a swallow,

swooping up into the blue.

It didn't last forever.
Just a few short, soaring minutes.

Soon, Dorothy was a Dorothy again,
heading home again.

"Did you go far, love?"

"Oh no, Dad. Not too far at all."

But she whispered
to the other children,
"It's true! It's true!"

◆

Colin Fox was next to go.
He walked straight up to Nanty Solo.
"Nanty Solo, I wish to be an eagle."
Nanty laughed.
"You'll never be an eagle.
You shall be a sparrow."
She made her marks.
She whispered her words.
Then she said,
"Go on. Be happy. Up you go."
In an instant, Colin was changed,
and off he flew.

Now lots of children wanted a turn.

Even Susan M'Beppe, just four years old.

She became a goldfinch.

Massive, muscly
Walter Pope
turned into
a rook.

Quiet Wolfgang Hurst
was transformed
into a parakeet.

Until one afternoon

the sky above the town

was filled with children who had turned into birds.

"No, no, no, no!"

"Get out of that sky this very minute!"

"Get back down here at once!"

"But what on earth are you frightened of?"

"Time to get rid of that Nanty Solo!"

"She's odd, she's bad, she's totally scary!"

"Bad Nanty Solo! Leave us alone!"

"Vamoose, skedaddle, scarper, scram."

◆

"OK, my dears. I'll be off.

I'm always on the move.

But perhaps you'd like, before I leave,

to have wings to fly

and a beak to sing."

◆

"What a silly crackpot notion!"

"Claptrap, tommyrot, piffle, bunkum!"

◆

"But what on earth are you frightened of?"

Oh look, it's the big feller,

Oswald Malone!

She's whispering her words

and making her marks.

And golly gumdrops, up he goes!

◆

"Gadzooks, what joy!

Hurrah, what fun!

Come on up! The sky's just grand!"

"Come on, Daddy! Come on, Teacher!
Come on, Officer Blenkinsop!"
Oh, just look and oh, just look.
Up they go and up they go.

Oh yes it's wild! It's simply silly!
Far out, barmy, dippy, kooky.
Nutty, freaky, batty, spooky.
"It's glorious! It's just the best!"

Now the sky is filled with joy.

The air is filled with such sweet song.

Up they go and up they go.

Up they go and up they go!

Nobody knows how Nanty did it.

Maybe she didn't know herself.

Soon enough she went away.

She goes to lots of towns they say.

And so that's that.

The story's done.

Go on. Be happy.

Off you fly.